For Dear Valley Readers
GO Reading!
Monica Wellington

Gabby & Grandma GO GREEN

Monica Wellington

Take care of trees.

Dutton Children's Books • An imprint of Penguin Group (USA) Inc.

For Lydia and her great-grandma, Gram Gram

The artwork was painted in gouache on paper, with color copies of photos cut out and pasted on.
The computer was not used in the preparation of this artwork.

THIS BOOK IS PRINTED ON ACID-FREE PAPER PRODUCED FROM RESPONSIBLY MANAGED FORESTS.

Dutton Children's Books
A division of Penguin Young Readers Group

Published by the Penguin Group
Penguin Group (USA) Inc., 375 Hudson Street, New York,
New York 10014, U.S.A. • Penguin Group (Canada), 90 Eglinton Avenue East, Suite 700, Toronto, Ontario M4P 2Y3, Canada
(a division of Pearson Penguin Canada Inc.) • Penguin Books Ltd, 80 Strand, London WC2R 0RL, England • Penguin Ireland, 25 St Stephen's Green,
Dublin 2, Ireland (a division of Penguin Books Ltd) • Penguin Group (Australia), 250 Camberwell Road, Camberwell, Victoria 3124, Australia (a division of
Pearson Australia Group Pty Ltd) • Penguin Books India Pvt Ltd, 11 Community Centre, Panchsheel Park, New Delhi - 110 017, India • Penguin Group (NZ),
67 Apollo Drive, Rosedale, North Shore 0632, New Zealand (a division of Pearson New Zealand Ltd) • Penguin Books (South Africa) (Pty) Ltd,
24 Sturdee Avenue, Rosebank, Johannesburg 2196, South Africa • Penguin Books Ltd, Registered Offices: 80 Strand, London WC2R 0RL, England

Text and illustrations copyright
© 2011 by Monica Wellington
All rights reserved.

CIP data available.

Published in the United States by Dutton Children's Books, • a division of Penguin Young Readers Group
345 Hudson Street, New York, New York 10014 • www.penguin.com/youngreaders

Designed by Abby Kuperstock
Manufactured in China • First Edition
ISBN: 978-0-525-42214-3
1 3 5 7 9 10 8 6 4 2

Bus
Stop

Our
Community
Garden

OUR GREEN PROJECTS:
Grow flowers
Sew reusable bags
Recycle bottles

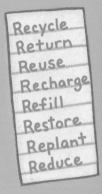

Recycle
Return
Reuse
Recharge
Refill
Restore
Replant
Reduce

When Gabby spends a day with her grandma, they love to do projects together. Gabby especially loves doing **GREEN** projects that are good for the Earth.

RECYCLE RECYCLE RECYCLE RECYCLE

seeds

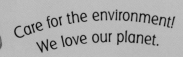

Care for the environment! We love our planet.

Let's recycle glass, plastic, and paper.

When Grandma gets out her sewing box,
Gabby wants to sew with Grandma's fabric.

Waste not, want not!

"Let's make reusable cloth bags," says Grandma.

They measure and cut.

See a pin and pick it up. All the day you'll have good luck!

They assemble and pin.

Side by side, they sew. They make their bags
sturdy and strong.

I remember when that fabric was a dress.

Shopping List:
Apples
Bread
Cat Food

go Green

PLEASE RECYCLE

earth-FRIENDLY

When their bags are finished, Gabby wants to use them right away! They fill them with plastic bottles to recycle and other things they need for their errands.

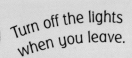

Turn off the lights when you leave.

Recycle more.
Throw away less.

REUSABLE
BAGS
HERE!

GREEN

greenplanet eco-

Earth Go Green

GO

At the supermarket they recycle their
bottles and shop for some groceries.
The clerk at the checkout counter asks,
"Paper or plastic?"
   "Not for us. We brought our own bags!"
says Gabby.

It's not trash when it
can be recycled.

OIDS NET 70 G

I'm sorting the bottles.

PLEASE
RECYCLE

Next stop—the Farmer's Market. There are fresh-picked fruits and vegetables, flowers, and many more things for sale.

"Let's buy some of our favorite foods," says Grandma.
"Thanks for buying local," says the farmer.

They pick out cheese and return their egg carton
to get more eggs.

Not a plastic bag in sight.

They buy bread and some yummy cookies. Their bags are heavy and full.

Save those scraps for compost.

WAX PAPER

Back in Grandma's kitchen, they wash
and dry, slice and cut. They make their
sandwiches, wrap them up, and are
ready to go.

Use cloth napkins
instead of paper.

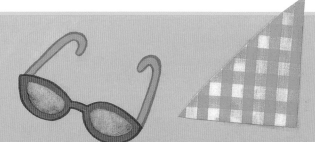

ONE DOZEN EGGS

In the park they find the perfect spot for a picnic.

"I wish I could feed the ducks," says Gabby. But she knows
the ducks have their own pond food to eat.

Green is fun.

While Gabby plays, Grandma reads her newspaper.

Recycle Paper

Save paper.
Save a tree.

Then Gabby recycles it. "Why, thank you," says Grandma.
Gabby says, "I have an idea where we should go next."

At the library they look for books with save the Earth projects. Gabby finds a book she likes and checks it out.

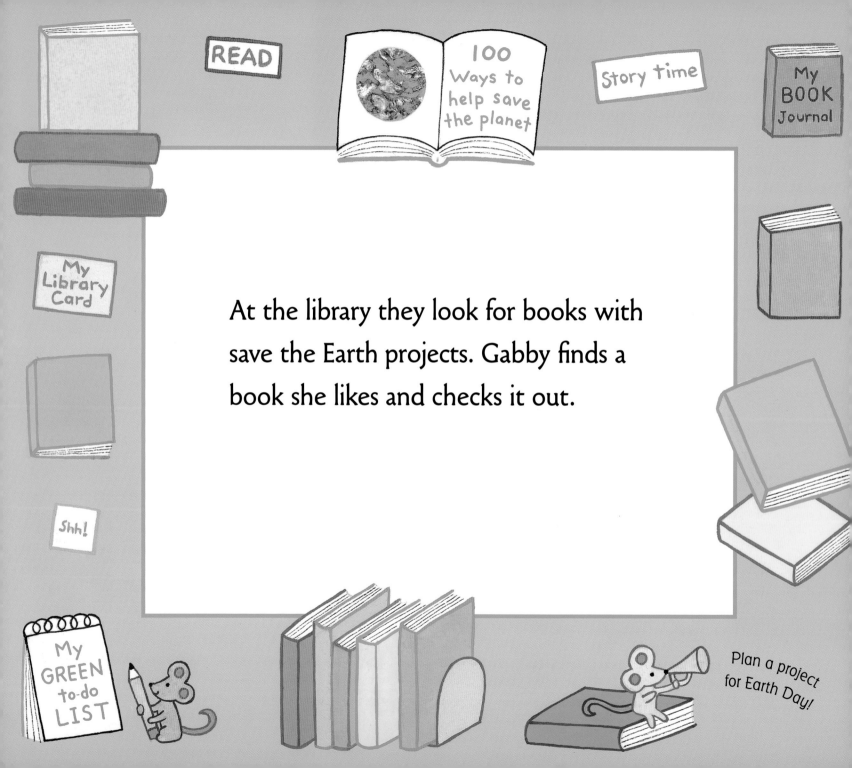

Library card

"We had a special **GREEN** Day with our bags," says Grandma.

"You and me together," says Gabby.

Hand in hand, they walk along to Grandma's home.

When they get back, Gabby wants to fill her bag
with fabric to take home.

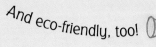

"I have ideas for lots of bags," says Gabby. "One will say *Go Green!*"

When Mom comes, Gabby says, "We had a great **GREEN** Day! And tomorrow, I'm going to sew a surprise for you!"

Green tips:
Change to long-life lightbulbs.

Don't let the water drip.
Draw on scrap paper.

recycle
reduce
reuse

Everyone can be green.
Every little bit helps!

Sewing a Cloth Bag

You can sew a cloth bag like Gabby, following these steps:

1. Choose a piece of fabric that is at least 12" x 24". (The exact size can vary, depending on what size bag you want to make.) You can buy a piece of fabric, but better yet, be like Gabby and Grandma and find fabric at home: cut up an old piece of clothing, old curtain, tablecloth, or pillowcase. Pick a strong cotton fabric. Discuss and choose (and get permission!) with an adult. You also need 1" wide strong ribbon for the strap for your bag.

2. Gather your tools: measuring tape, scissors, pins, needle, and thread.

3. Measure and cut the 12" x 24" piece from your fabric. You can mark the fabric with chalk and then cut along the lines.

4. Then fold the 24" length of fabric in half, with right side of fabric together. Pin the two side seams together.

5. Stitch the two seams using a basic straight running stitch. Sew half inch in from the edge. Press seam open.

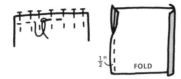

6. Turn over the top edge 1" and pin in place. Use the basic straight stitch to sew this hem.

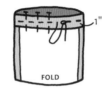

7. Cut an 18" length of ribbon. Place the ribbon on either side of the bag, on the inside of the bag. Pin into place and sew securely, as shown.

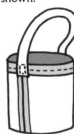

8. Turn the bag right side out and your bag is finished, sturdy and strong! There are many variations possible. You can make your bag bigger or smaller, with the strap longer or shorter. Have fun making a bag all your own!

Green Tips

- Plant a community garden! It's fun for all and great for the environment.

- Use your own bags at the grocery store.

- Riding bicycles and buses cuts down on car pollution.

- Conserve water—don't leave it running.

- When packing a lunch, use wax paper instead of plastic wrap.

- Use silverware instead of disposable plastic ware.

- Make sure to throw trash in the proper receptacles—don't litter.

- A recycled tire makes a great tire swing!

- Recycle your paper and save trees

- Plan a project on Earth Day, like planting a tree or picking up litter in a park.

- You can donate or recycle or hand down your clothes when you're done with them.

- Use rechargeable batteries in all your toys and electronics.

- Eco-friendly lightbulbs are more energy efficient, so they last a lot longer!

For more information, visit:

www.epa.gov/kids
www.nrdc.org/greensquad
www.planetpals.com